A Coloring & Activ

ax & Ruby

Max & Ruby Celebrate Easter

Grosset & Dunlap
An Imprint of Penguin Group (USA) Inc.

Based upon the animated series *Max & Ruby*
A Nelvana Limited production © 2002–2003.

The publisher does not have any control over and does not assume
any responsibility for author or third-party websites or their content.

ISBN 978-0-448-45270-8   1 0 9 8 7 6

It's springtime!
Ruby is picking pretty flowers in the garden.

The Easter Bunny wants to take an Easter surprise to Max & Ruby's house. But he's lost. Can you help him find his way?

START

FINISH

Ruby shows Grandma her favorite Easter egg.

Use these steps to draw a flower.

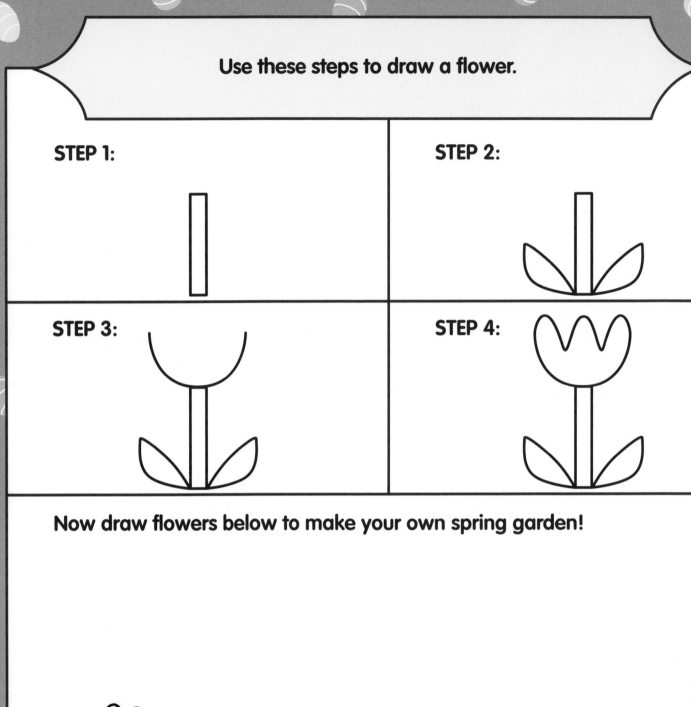

STEP 1:

STEP 2:

STEP 3:

STEP 4:

Now draw flowers below to make your own spring garden!

Max has to figure out which color comes next. Can you help him? Color what comes next.

Create your own colorful Easter egg!
You can use the stickers in this book to decorate your egg.

Use these stickers on page 9.

Ruby has to put eggs in all of these baskets.
Can you help her? Use your stickers to put the correct
number of eggs in each basket. Then trace each number.

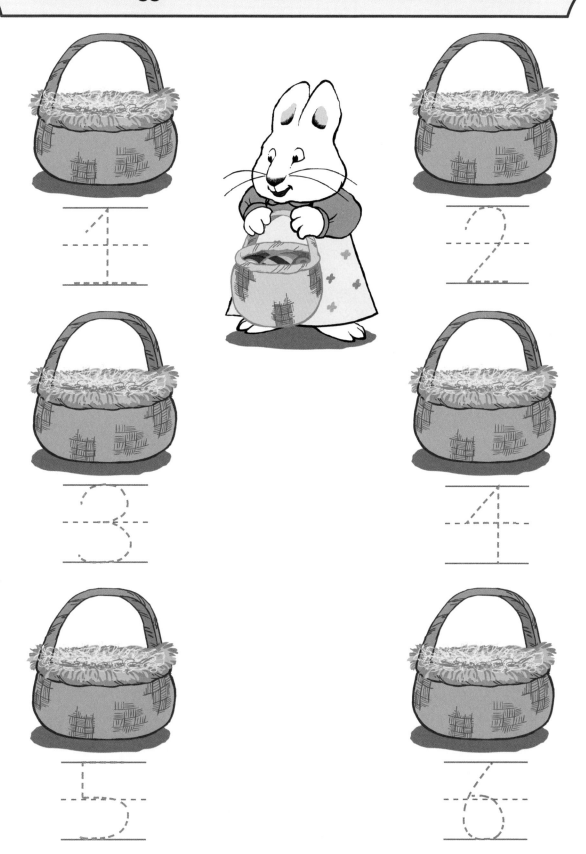

1

2

3

4

5

6

Color the picture that is different in each row.

Max made a new friend—and he's very *springy*!

Draw lines to match the pictures that rhyme.

Connect the dots to find out what Max does to help his flowers grow!

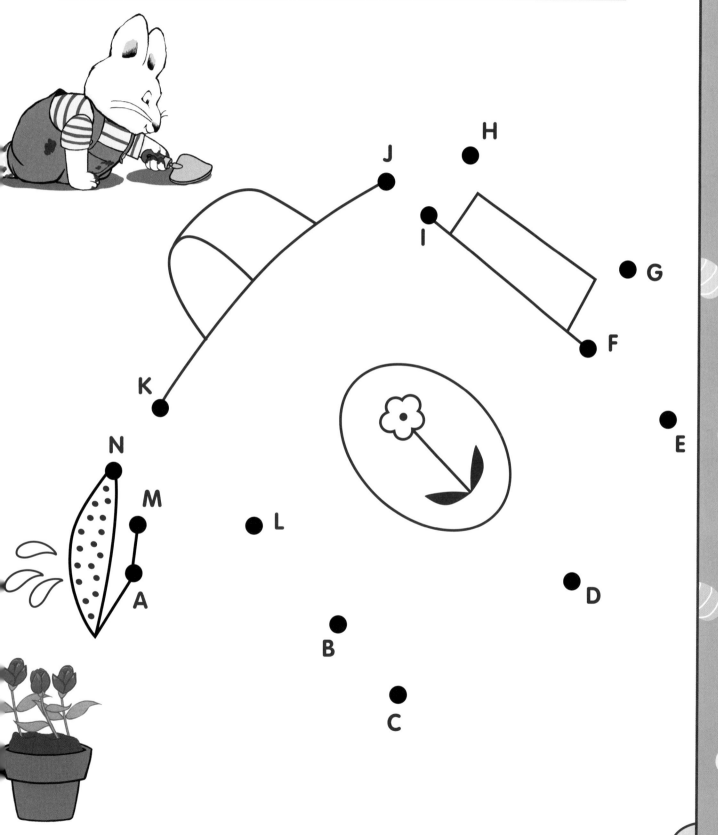

Max loves to write! Help him practice writing the letters that spell *Easter*. Then, trace the special Easter message at the bottom of the page!

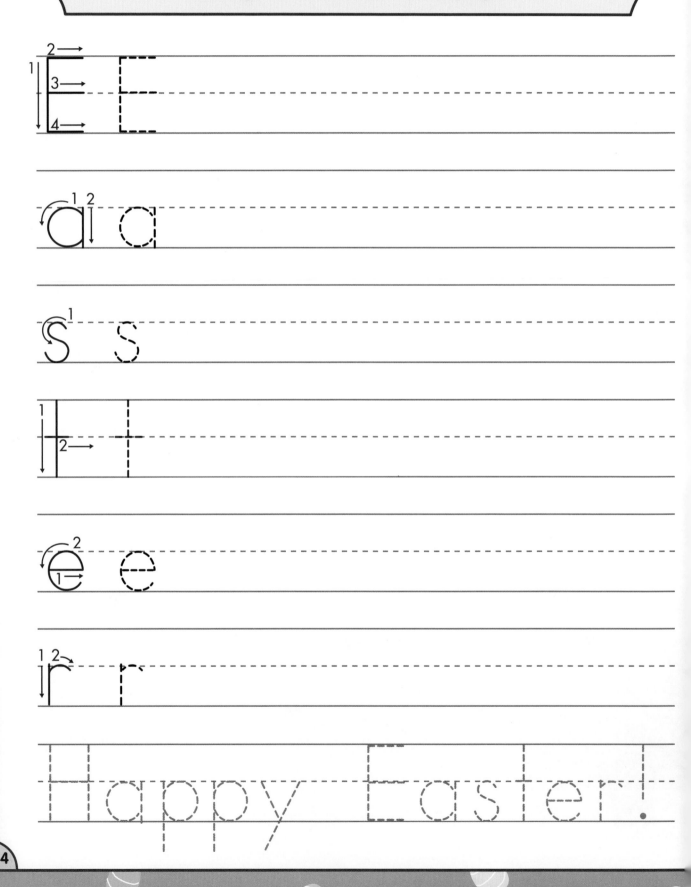

Happy Easter from Max and Ruby!

ANSWERS:

Page 3:

Page 7:

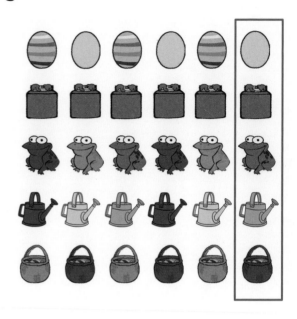

Page 10:

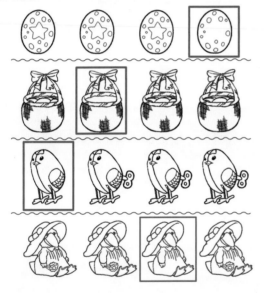

Page 12:

Page 13:

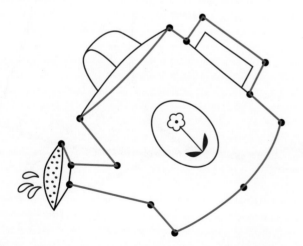